# Toads and Diamonds

retold and illustrated by

## Robert Bender

**Lodestar Books**

Dutton    New York

*dedicated from this toad to*
*his one and only precious jewel*

## Author's Note

*Toads and Diamonds*, originally called *Les Fées* (*The Fairies*), first appeared in Charles Perrault's 1697 storybook titled *Histoires, ou contes du temps passé* (*Tales of Times Past*). In the frontispiece of that edition were the words *Contes de ma mère l'Oyé*, which translates into the now famous title *Mother Goose Tales*. Included in that collection are *Sleeping Beauty, Cinderella, Little Red Riding Hood, Puss in Boots,* and a relatively obscure tale on which I based this book.

There once lived a nasty widow named Asphalta, and only her breath was more foul than the words she spoke. She had two daughters, Bleacha and Merth. Bleacha was a chip off her mother's horrible block, while Merth had grown into a kind and generous young woman.

Merth was also quite beautiful. So Asphalta and Bleacha, in their jealous rage, would punish her with cruel tricks and harsh demands.

On one cold dark night, Asphalta and Bleacha decided that
they wanted hot chocolate, but they had no water in the kettle.
Turning their greedy eyes toward Merth, they commanded,
"Fetch us some water from the well on the far side of the hill!"

Merth dreaded wandering off into the scary dark night, but at least she could escape for a while from her mother and sister.

As she whistled to forget the cold wind, birds swooped out of the trees and surprised her with songs of their own.

Merth was having such a good time that she didn't notice the log that sent her sprawling onto the path.

When she sat up and rubbed her eyes, she saw that it was no log at all.

Three sets of eyes looked at her and three mouths spoke in unison: "Please don't run from our ugly faces! We are just a harmless, homely, three-headed troll. If you would be so kind as to comb our matted hair and brush the moss off our noses, our lives will be put back in order again."

That seems easy enough, thought Merth, and she proceeded to clean them up.

As if the three-headed troll had read her mind, it replied, "It would be easy to run from such a sight as us. You are the first in many years to do a kind task on our behalf. As a reward, every time you sing, only the most precious jewels will come from your mouth!"

Merth could not believe it was true, but
in case it was, she decided to sing "Thank you
very much" in her sweetest voice. The moment
she uttered those words, a sparkling diamond
popped out of her mouth.

When Merth rushed home (forgetting the water), Asphalta and Bleacha immediately noticed the gem glistening through her pocket lining.

"From whose treasure chest did you steal this gem?" accused Asphalta.

"She probably dug it up from somebody's grave," added Bleacha.

To this, Merth simply sang "I did not steal it" in her most bittersweet voice.

As she spoke, precious jewels poured from her mouth. Before her mother and sister had a chance to make any more cruel remarks, Merth escaped into her room.

Asphalta pierced Bleacha with her greedy eyes and said, "Go to that well this instant and find the cause of these riches! We must also get what we deserve!"

Bleacha resented having to journey out into the cold night, riches or no riches. She kicked stones and grumbled as she made her way along the path. No bird dared to flutter by or even let out a chirp.

Getting angrier with each passing moment, she kicked bigger stones and logs with all her might.

Finally, she kicked a big, soggy old log. The log didn't budge, but Bleacha went flying into the dirt.

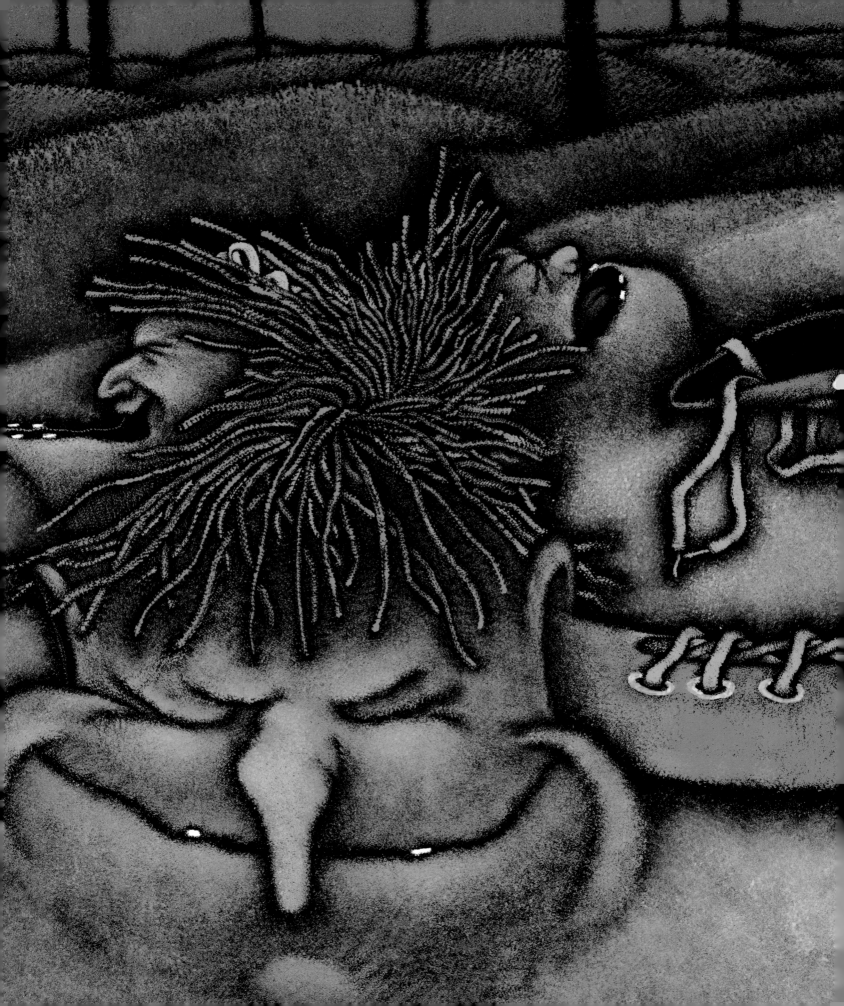

When she sat up and wiped the mud off her cheeks, she saw the very same troll that Merth had stumbled across. And her boot was sticking into one of its ears!

All at once the troll said, "Good lady, after you remove your boot from our ear, would you be so kind as to comb our matted hair and wipe the moss from our noses?"

Bleacha let out such a horrible screech that even the three-headed troll had to close all six of its eyes for a moment.

As she grabbed her boot, Bleacha said, "You are the most loathsome, horrible creature I have ever seen. The only thing that I would do for you is to bury your ugly heads with sticks and leaves!"

In a calm but firm voice, the troll replied, "Only nasty and vile words pass from your lips, so from now on, whenever you speak, nothing but slimy toads, vipers, and insects will drop from your mouth!"

When Bleacha opened her mouth to protest, a big, belching toad flopped out.

Bewildered and panic-stricken, she raced off into the woods, not caring in which direction she went.

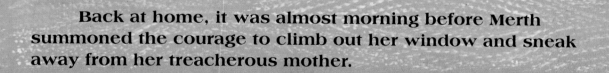

Back at home, it was almost morning before Merth
summoned the courage to climb out her window and sneak
away from her treacherous mother.

Merth wandered down the first path she could find. As she thought about what to do next, she began to sing.

With the first line of her song, along came seven shining trinkets of gold.

Suddenly, it was obvious what she could do. Merth hurried off toward the nearby town.

By the time she arrived, Merth's pockets were stuffed
with jewels because she'd been singing all the way there. The
curious townsfolk gathered around her to marvel at her riches.

After hearing her story of enchantment, everyone agreed that Merth should be treated as a queen. The townspeople built a castle for her to live in. That is where she joyfully spent the rest of her days, making song and many riches. And she was always as generous with her jewels as she was with her music, so the peasants, too, felt like nobles.

Back at home, Asphalta was left with nobody to order around, so she spent the rest of her days yelling at the chairs, tables, and walls in her house.

As for Bleacha, no one ever saw her again.
Rumor had it that she lived in a shadowy part of
the forest where there seemed to be an especially
large population of toads, vipers, and insects.